GREAT GRANDMA'S
ASTONISHING ADVENTURES

By Lois Davis

Strategic Book Publishing and Rights Co.

Strategic Book Publishing and Rights Co.
12620 FM 1960, Suite A4-507
Houston, TX 77065
www.sbpra.com

ISBN: 978-1-62857-459-3

Book Design: Suzanne Kelly

DEDICATION

*This book is dedicated to my darling Dad, who has given me
the wonderful gift of storytelling, and who would have been so proud.*

Lois Davis

ACKNOWLEDGEMENTS

Love and thanks go to my wonderful family and friends. Your encouragement, support, and belief in me is total, and has meant so much to me. I have loved every minute of this journey in becoming an author. I feel what I write, as a musician feels his music.

The inspiration for this book comes from my Mum, and my twin grandchildren Luisa and Rafael who live in Brazil. That though, is a story in itself!

Special thanks must go to my darling husband Keith. All your love and support has enabled me to make this happen.

To my dear Mum, your pride in me, and that you are here to see this, means so much. I am so grateful for being able to have the benefit of your advice.

To my dear sister Lindsay, your enthusiasm for my work knows no bounds, and is, in itself, so motivating. The fact that you can see Dad in my work is very special to me. It doesn't seem possible that we have been without him for twenty five years.

To my newly-found sister-in-law Pat (yes, there is a story there too!) for your love and practical advice where it is needed most.

To my children, Nicholas, Simone, Tanya, and Hannah, you all believe in me, and I know I have made each one of you, near or far, very proud.

All my grandchildren are special, but it would be remiss of me not to thank my eldest grandchild Amelie. Yours was the inspiration for the rug in the castle, the sage and lavender scones, and that you thought my work was, in your own words, "amazing!" Who needs book reviews! Sometimes, you are way beyond your six years.

Special thanks go to Daire (you are a star) and to Marilyn. Thank you both for all your efforts, support, and enthusiasm for my work. Marilyn, your generosity of spirit, and of your time, never wanting any thanks, makes you very special. I will never forget how much of yourself you have given me to enable me to make this happen. You were surely sent from heaven.

To Jean, Chanie, and Laura for your inspirational insight, thank you all for your love and encouragement which means so much.

And last, but by no means least, thanks go to Tom, Lynn, Bruce, Vern, and Helen at SBPRA, my agent and publisher. Special thanks must go to Suzanne, for you have done such a brilliant job. To you all, I greatly value your help, guidance, and patience.

CONTENTS

INTRODUCTION

There is a message conveyed throughout my writing. It is one of helping others, consideration, safety, kindness, forgiveness, honesty, encouragement and pride, and fun! There is also an educational element to my storytelling.

I feel this is all so needed in today's world.

—Lois Davis

GREAT GRANDMA AND THE FLYING PANCAKES

CHAPTER 1

Great Grandma raised her head from the pillow. "Oh dear, oh dear," she groaned, "I feel sooooo poorly."

She lay her head back down, and turned to Mincemeat, her extremely large ginger cat who lay curled up cosily on the old red armchair next to Great Grandma's bed. Mincemeat was no ordinary cat, for he was a magic cat. He could fly through the air, and he was just amazing at

tap dancing! But most of all Mincemeat just loved cooking! He also loved cream and cream cheese!

Great Grandma groaned again. Mincemeat was much too comfy to bother even turning his lovely, ginger head. Instead he regarded Great Grandma with his twinkly brown eyes and gave a massive sigh. *I expect Great Grandma wants me to make her a cup of tea,* he thought to himself. But Mincemeat loved Great Grandma so much, he really didn't mind.

"Mincemeat, please can you pass me the telephone," Great Grandma said. "I shall have to ring the doctor."

Mincemeat was a very kindly cat, and because he knew the doctor's telephone number off by heart, he dialled the number for her. The telephone in Doctor Wobblebottom's surgery rang for quite a few minutes before he answered. *He must be very busy today,* Great Grandma thought. Then, a minute later, "Good morning, this is Doctor Wobblebottom speaking, how can I help you?"

"Oh, Good morning Doctor Wobblebottom, this is Great Grandma speaking. I feel sooooo poorly, I can't imagine what is wrong with me."

"What did you have for supper?" asked Doctor Wobblebottom.

"Oh, what I usually have on a Tuesday evening if it's raining. I had two crispy fried spiders on toast with a stinging nettle salad, and a very large bowl of rain water and mud soup."

"I don't think that any of that could have upset your tummy," replied Doctor Wobblebottom. "But I think I had better come and see you anyway."

"Thank you so much," said Great Grandma. "Mincemeat will open the door for you."

Sometime later, when Doctor Wobblebottom had finished seeing all his patients at his surgery, he set out in his lovely old car to see Great Grandma. Doctor Wobblebottom's car was his pride and joy. His steering wheel was made of old spaghetti, and wobbled about in his hands.

Doctor Wobblebottom had to travel along a very long and thin winding lane called Roast Potato Lane to reach Great Grandma's cottage, which stood at the top of a hill. Doctor Wobblebottom's little old car bounced all down the lane, for it was full of old roast potatoes as you would expect from its name! The Doctor finally arrived at the bottom of the lane where the hill began. He parked his car under a big old oak tree and started to climb the hill towards Great Grandma's cottage. He huffed and puffed his way up clutching onto his doctor's bag which was full of magic potions.

As Doctor Wobblebottom climbed the hill, a big rain cloud appeared in the sky and, soon enough, giant rain drops the size of saucers began to plop out of the sky right on to the Doctor's nose. *Oh dear, oh dear,* thought Doctor Wobblebottom, I had better get my umbrella out. As he put his umbrella up, a huge gust of wind whipped up under his coat and his umbrella, and he was whisked up into the air. He was flying through the air, higher and higher, and faster and faster, clutching his doctor's bag as tightly as he could. Doctor Wobblebottom flew right over Great

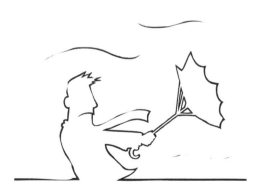

Grandma's cottage and, all of a sudden, the wind and the huge rain drops stopped. With a great big thump, the Doctor was plonked right on top of Great Grandma's chimney pot! Or so he thought, for Doctor Wobblebottom was a man shaped like a pudding, and he was actually wedged tight fast in the chimney pot!

CHAPTER 2

Doctor Wobblebottom squeezed and pushed and tried with all his strength to lift himself up out of the chimney, but he seemed to be stuck fast. Down in the cottage, he could hear Mincemeat practising his tap dancing.

Doctor Wobblebottom tried calling out, "Help, please help, it's Doctor Wobblebottom and I am stuck in the chimney!"

But Mincemeat had the music for his tap dancing practice on so loud that neither Great Grandma nor Mincemeat could hear him.

Well, thought Doctor Wobblebottom, *there is only one thing for it. I will have to make myself as thin as possible.* With that, he sucked in all his breath and, all of a sudden and with a great big loud whoosh, slid down the chimney as fast as lightning and landed with a huge plop right in Great Grandma's fireplace. Of course he was covered from head to toe in soot, and there were great clouds of soot all over Great Grandma's sitting room.

Mincemeat almost jumped out of his skin as the Doctor whooshed down the chimney and landed with a great big thump in the fireplace. Then Mincemeat saw the funny side of it and started laughing uncontrollably until the tears ran down his lovely ginger furry face. Of course, whilst all this was going on downstairs in the sitting room, Great Grandma was still upstairs in bed waiting for Doctor Wobblebottom's visit.

Doctor Wobblebottom got to his feet and started to dust himself off. Clouds of soot wafted about the room and settled everywhere. *Oh my golly,* Mincemeat thought to himself, *Great Grandma is not going to be pleased when she sees all this mess.* The Doctor rescued his bag with all his magic

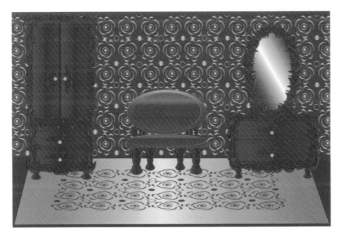

potions in it from the fireplace and, leaving the sitting room, he started to climb the stairs to see Great Grandma. Great Grandma was by now sitting in bed propped up on a mountain of pillows which Mincemeat had lovingly arranged for her.

She took one look at the state of Doctor Wobblebottom and said in a very shrill voice, "Oh my goodness gracious, whatever has happened to you?!"

The Doctor sat on the end of Great Grandma's bed and proceeded to tell her all about his adventure. She could hardly believe her ears. When the Doctor had finished, he asked Great Grandma how she was feeling. She told him that she felt sooooo poorly, and, so opening his bag, he took out his magic stethoscope to listen to her heart beat. Putting it on her chest, he could not believe what he was hearing, for Great Grandma's heart was clanging away like a great big orchestra! Then Doctor Wobblebottom put the stethoscope on her tummy, and that was clanging away like a great big fire engine siren! The Doctor was quiet for a few minutes.

"Whatever do you think is the matter with me?" asked Great Grandma.

CHAPTER 3

Well, what fun was going on inside Great Grandma!!

Geoffrey the Germ and Billy the Bug were having a fantastic time! They were climbing up Great Grandma's insides and whizzing back down again. They were tickling her bones and blowing trumpets and clanging cymbals as loudly as they possibly could, and laughing and laughing and laughing until they fell about completely exhausted! Doctor Wobblebottom scratched his head and thought.

"I think" he ventured slowly, "that the best thing to do, is that you should sit in bed with two pancakes on your head for at least a week, and I do believe that will do the trick. Unfortunately, I do not possess a magic potion for clanging. I will come back and see you in a week's time," he said to Great Grandma. "Meanwhile, so that you will feel better, I will give Mincemeat some pink potion to put inside the pancakes, but it is all I have left and I can't get any more."

Downstairs, Mincemeat was hoovering up all the soot and polishing everything in Great Grandma's sitting room until it all gleamed bright and shiny. *I can't possibly let Great Grandma see all this mess,* he thought to himself, and he set about his work with great gusto. He had put some music on to help him whilst he worked, for he so loved dancing.

Doctor Wobblebottom came downstairs and, entering the sitting room, he saw Mincemeat dancing the most beautiful dance whilst pushing the Hoover and humming along with the music.

"Mincemeat," said Doctor Wobblebottom, "I need you to make some pancakes please. Great Grandma needs to sit with them on top of her head in order to get better. I will return in a week and hope to find Great Grandma as fit as a fiddle."

Giving Mincemeat the pink potion, and explaining that he could not get any more, Doctor Wobblebottom saw himself out of the cottage, and began climbing down the hill to where he had left his car at the bottom under the big oak tree.

Mincemeat put the Hoover and the polish neatly away, and, fluffing up the cushions on the sofa, he left the sitting room to set to in the kitchen. He climbed up carefully onto a rather high stool to reach the cupboard where Great Grandma kept all her cooking ingredients, and fetched them out. Then climbing back down, he put on his 'I Love Cooking' apron, and began to make the pancakes for Great Grandma. He sang whilst he worked, for Mincemeat was a very happy cat. Soon there were delicious smells wafting from the kitchen all around the cottage, and Great Grandma thought she felt very hungry indeed. As Mincemeat busied himself, he sang a little rhyme:

"Two pancakes for her head, whilst sitting in her bed, another for her nose and jam ones for her toes!"

Mincemeat felt very pleased with himself indeed, and puffed out his ginger furry chest with immense pride.

A short while later, Mincemeat put two of the pancakes on Great Grandma's favourite plate which was decorated with slugs. Putting the plate on a wooden tray, he slowly climbed the stairs. Great Grandma had fallen asleep sitting up in bed against her mountain of pillows. Her silver grey curly hair framed her round face and her nose looked more pointy than usual. Mincemeat shook her very gently with his large ginger paw to wake her up, and her sparkly blue eyes opened. Very carefully, Mincemeat placed two of the pancakes, just as Doctor Wobblebottom had instructed, on top of Great Grandma's head. There were two pancakes left on the plate, and Mincemeat had filled those with squashed tomatoes and fried dandelions knowing it was one of Great Grandma's favourite meals. She tucked in hungrily, and it made Mincemeat very happy to see her enjoy the pancakes that he had made with so much love.

CHAPTER 4

A few days later, early one morning, and just as the sun was rising in the sky, Great Grandma said to Mincemeat, "Do you know, I think I am beginning to feel very much better indeed."

Mincemeat was so pleased and he drew back her bright pink curtains decorated with spiders' webs, letting the sunshine stream in through the windows. He then thought it would be a very good idea for Great Grandma to have some lovely fresh air all around her bedroom, and so, with a great flourish, he threw open the windows. Just at that minute a huge gust of wind blew in, and all of a sudden the two pancakes sitting on top of Great Grandma's head flew off and out of the window!

Oh no! thought Mincemeat, *whatever am I going to do?* He saw the pancakes hanging from the highest branch of the horse chestnut tree in the cottage garden. Mincemeat knew he could not fly that high, and that he would never be able to reach them. He also remembered Doctor Wobblebottom telling him there was no more of the pink potion to put inside the pancakes!

What will I do, what will I do? Mincemeat thought to himself.

In the meantime, inside Great Grandma, Geoffrey the Germ and Billy the Bug were just waking up from a very long sleep.

"I'm bored," complained Geoffrey.

"Well then," said Billy, "let's have some fun!! Let's climb right up inside Great Grandma's nose and tickle it" said Billy, ".....and make her sneeze and sneeze!" suggested Geoffrey. And that's just what they did! Geoffrey and Billy climbed higher and higher inside Great Grandma's nose and tickled and tickled and tickled it until she sneezed and sneezed and sneezed. And Geoffrey and Billy laughed and laughed and laughed until they fell about completely exhausted!

But then suddenly everything changed for Billy and Geoffrey, for they tickled Great Grandma's nose so much that she sneezed so hard, and out flew Billy and Geoffrey, who landed with a great thud upon the window sill. They were not having so much fun anymore.

Great Grandma regarded them sternly from where she sat in bed and said, "Now you two, would you like to tell me just what has been going on!"

Billy and Geoffrey sat very very still. They were frightened. After all the fun they had had, they now came face to face with Great Grandma. They had never imagined they would. It was scary!

Billy, being the braver of the two, spoke first, "We are really really sorry that we have made you feel so poorly. We really didn't mean it, it's just that we were having so much fun, and then we had some more fun, and then we just could not stop....." "....having fun" said Geoffrey in a very small voice. "We realise we were being very naughty," they both said together, "and we promise that we will never do it again."

"We would like to make it up to you Great Grandma, please let us," said Geoffrey, who was now feeling a little bit braver.

"Well, I will have to think about all this very carefully," said Great Grandma, still regarding them sternly. "In the meantime, you will have to sleep under the large dock leaf by the wishing well in the garden, and I will see both of you again in the morning."

CHAPTER 5

Geoffrey and Billy could not sleep. They were feeling very sad about having made Great Grandma so poorly. They sat up all night chatting about how they could make amends.

Upstairs, Mincemeat stretched his arms and legs, where he had been curled up sleeping on the old red armchair next to Great Grandma's bed. He yawned a huge yawn. *Time to get up,* he thought. *Great Grandma needs a nice cup of tea, and I think I need to check on those two naughty boys under the dock leaf in the garden.* Mincemeat padded down the stairs on his large paws. Switching on the radio, he did a little dance round the kitchen with the old broom that stood propped up in the corner by the large kitchen stove, twirling this way and that, and swaying in time to the music. Filling the kettle with water, he lit the gas stove, and put the kettle on to boil. A few minutes later the kettle loudly whistled, telling Mincemeat that he could now make the tea. Mincemeat stretched up to the shelf and took down a large round white teapot and spooned some tea leaves into it. Lifting the kettle from the stove, he then very very carefully poured the water in to make the tea. Opening the biscuit tin, he took out two biscuits that he had baked with freshly dead flies the day before, and which Great Grandma just loved! Mincemeat had gathered the dead flies from the greenhouse himself, and dusted them with icing sugar before adding them to the biscuit mixture. He was so proud of himself for making up such a delicious recipe! Putting the biscuits on a plate, he then put it on the wooden tray together with a cup of tea, and tottered up the stairs.

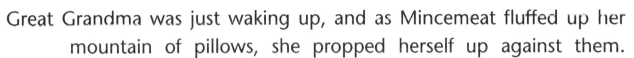

Great Grandma was just waking up, and as Mincemeat fluffed up her mountain of pillows, she propped herself up against them. Leaving the tea and biscuits on the rather rickety side table for her, he went back downstairs to listen to the news on the radio. Padding down the garden path, Mincemeat went to see Billy and Geoffrey.

Mincemeat lifted the huge dock leaf by the wishing well. Geoffrey was crying, and Billy had his arm round him comforting him.

"Whatever is the matter?" asked Mincemeat.

"We just know that Gr.. Gr.. Great Grandma is not going to forgive us," Geoffrey sobbed.

"Of course she will," encouraged Mincemeat, and kindly giving Geoffrey his black and white spotted handkerchief to dry his eyes, he said "now don't be sad. I have a plan!"

CHAPTER 6

Soon, back in the cottage there was great excitement in the kitchen, as Mincemeat went about organizing his plan. They were going to make Great Grandma a wonderful surprise by baking a beetle and apple pie for her! One of Great Grandma's favourites!

Billy and Geoffrey were busy helping. Geoffrey was chopping apples, whilst Billy helped Mincemeat to make the pastry by spooning the flour into the bowl. When the pie was prepared, Mincemeat very carefully put it in the oven to bake. Soon Great Grandma's nose was filled with the delicious smell of the pie baking. *Oooh!* she thought to herself, *I wonder what Mincemeat is up to now? What a very delicious smell!*

The pie was soon ready, and Mincemeat very carefully took it out of the oven with his oven gloves. He put a beautiful tray cloth made of dandelion leaves onto the wooden tray.

Then putting the pie on the tray, Mincemeat said to Billy and Geoffrey, "Now you two, sit on the tray and hold the pie steady please!"

Billy and Geoffrey were smiling. It felt good to be making Great Grandma happy. Climbing the stairs, Mincemeat carried the tray with them and the pie on it, up to Great Grandma's bedroom.

When she saw what they had done, Great Grandma could not stay cross with them any longer. She was feeling so much better, and she could see that Billy and Geoffrey were truly sorry. Soon they were all tucking in to the most delicious pie they had ever tasted.

"I think I will get up today," declared Great Grandma. "I think," she said to Mincemeat, "it is time for an adventure!"

Mincemeat beamed. He was quite ready for an adventure with Great Grandma. He would quite like a little rest from dusting and baking.

And so that is just what they did!

GREAT GRANDMA AND THE MAGIC RASPBERRY

CHAPTER 1

Great Grandma was very old, but also very rascally. It was time for an adventure!

The Magic Raspberry was kept under the huge weeping willow tree by the wishing well in the garden. Mincemeat, Great Grandma's very lovely and very large ginger cat, was busying himself polishing the Magic Raspberry ready for the adventure, until it gleamed so brightly he could see his beautiful ginger face in its reflection. The Raspberry was indeed magic, for it could fly in the sky and sail on the ocean. Mincemeat was getting everything ready. Great Grandma had told Mincemeat that she wanted to take her best china tea set with them, and so he was wrapping it very carefully in big dock leaves picked from the garden, before putting it in the suitcase. He had polished Great Grandma's black boots that morning until they shone, and put them in the suitcase. He also put in two huge juicy meat and potato pies that he wrapped in a large black and white spotted handkerchief. Mincemeat had baked the pies specially that morning for, as you know, he was a cat who loved cooking! He then put in two nettle cakes, two beetle and apple pies, a tin of dead fly biscuits, and three large bunches of fried dandelions, in fact, all of Great Grandma's favourite things. Finally, Mincemeat put in two big bottles of blackberry squash and a bottle of parsnip juice. He then loaded the suitcase inside the Magic Raspberry.

Mincemeat washed the bright pink wheels of the Magic Raspberry with dandelion juice and polished them lovingly. He then went to the greenhouse to find an enormous cosy yellow spotted rug, which he spread out inside the Magic Raspberry. The steering wheel was made of old sausages, and the engine was made of lots of old fish fingers and chips and old wheel cogs, and worked very well.

Mincemeat went back up the garden path to the cottage, to sweep the floors and to make sure that everything was clean and tidy before they left. Upstairs, Great Grandma was getting ready. She had decorated her curly silver grey hair with bluebells from the garden (which matched the colour of her sparkly blue eyes) and her blue jumper and skirt were made from the softest dormouse wool you would ever feel.

Locking the front door of the cottage, Great Grandma then put the key under the huge flowerpot that stood by the front door.

It seemed that everything was ready for the adventure to begin!

CHAPTER 2

Far far away on an island in the South China Sea in a castle, lived Clive the Crocodile. It was a very fine castle with a very pointy roof and lots and lots of windows, some very small, and some very big. It had a very tall wooden front door. All around the castle was a race track! Clive loved racing cars!

Clive lived alone in his castle, and I shall tell you just how he came to live there.

One sunny day, when there was not a cloud to be seen in the very blue sky, Clive the Crocodile had found the castle quite by chance. He had been swimming all morning, enjoying the day, and suddenly he came upon the island. There, in the sunlight, shone the castle! *Oh goodness me, jumping alligators,* thought Clive, *what a beautiful castle!* He came out of the sea and onto the island. He walked all around the island looking at the castle from this way and that. Clive ventured up the long path which led to the front door. Hanging on a very long piece of rope was a large shiny brass bell which Clive rang. He waited. No answer. He rang the bell again. Still no answer. As he was thinking to himself that he would try just once more, he noticed that the front door was open very very slightly.

Clive gently pushed open the door which was much heavier than it looked. "Hello" called out Clive. "Is there anybody home?" There was no reply. He tried again "Helloooooooooooooo. Is there anybody there?" The castle was completely silent. *I think I shall have to have a little explore,* Clive thought to himself.

He went into a lovely lounge, where there was a large red brick fireplace for lighting a log fire on chilly winter evenings. The walls were decorated with all different sea shells. On the floor, was a cosy bright

blue and red round rug. There were two red comfy armchairs placed each side of the fireplace, and a large red sofa opposite. By now, Clive was feeling rather tired after all his swimming and finding the castle, and so he decided to stretch out on the sofa to have a snooze.

CHAPTER 3

When Clive woke up everything was in darkness. *I must have been asleep a jolly long time,* he thought, and indeed he had. He had been exhausted. He stretched his long body, and made his way up the very long winding staircase that led from the hall opposite the front door. Luckily, the moonlight was very bright, and the moonbeams danced in through the castle windows so that Clive could see where he was going. Upstairs, he found a bedroom with a lovely bed that had upon it a huge white duvet made from the softest feathers in the world. Next door to the bedroom was a great big bathroom that had the biggest bath in it that Clive had ever seen. *Jumping alligators,* thought Clive, *I think that bath is bigger than the South China Sea!* He was so excited, for if there was anything that Clive loved to do, it was sloshing about in a bath with millions and millions and trillions of bubbles! And guess what, there on the side of the bath was a tall green bottle with the words 'Scrubbly Bubbly Bubble Bath'. Clive clapped his hands together, he was so happy!

He decided to run himself a lovely bath, and poured the bubble bath in carefully. Then he lay in all the bubbles for quite a long while whistling to himself. Stepping out of the bath, Clive reached for a large fluffy white bath towel from the rack to dry himself off. When he was dry, he hung it neatly back on the rack. By this time, Clive was feeling rather peckish, and so he climbed down the staircase to see where the kitchen was. It was on the opposite side of the hall to the lounge. Inside the kitchen he found a large old cooker, a big sink, several cupboards, a tall fridge, and a square kitchen table with four wooden chairs. Two of the chairs were large, and the other two were smaller. *Thank goodness the moon is bright tonight,* thought Clive, because it meant that he could see everything clearly. He would be finding out tomorrow that there were no lights in the castle, only candles, which he would have to be very careful lighting. Opening the fridge, Clive found three lettuce leaves, half a cucumber, and two crispy green apples. *Well,* he thought, *those lettuce leaves are not going to fill me up very much,* but sitting down at the kitchen table on one of the larger chairs, he munched on the lettuce leaves anyway, together with the cucumber and the apples.

All of a sudden, something caught his eye on the table. It was a note written in big bold writing. It said:

CASTLE FOR SALE, PLEASE ENQUIRE AT THE COTTAGE ON THE OTHER SIDE OF THE ISLAND AND ASK FOR MALCOLM.

Clive could not believe his eyes. *Right* he said to himself, *first thing in the morning I shall see about this!* By now, Clive felt that he needed a good night's sleep in that lovely bed with the snugly duvet, and so he climbed upstairs. He lay down on the bed, he was oh so comfy, and soon fast asleep.

CHAPTER 4

The very next morning, the first thing Clive did, was climb out of bed to make his way downstairs and out of the castle to find Malcolm, who turned out to be Malcolm the Macaw, a very brightly coloured parrot. His colours of red, yellow and blue, were truly breathtaking. Clive knocked on the door of the cottage, and when Malcolm opened it Clive was amazed to see such a beautiful parrot. Clive gave a little bow for he wanted to be extra polite.

"Do come in" said Malcolm. "What can I do for you?"

Clive said, "Are you Malcolm?"

"I am indeed, and who might you be?" Malcolm enquired questioningly.

"I, Sir, am Clive, and I am very happy to meet you. I have discovered the castle, and it seems that it is up for sale. I would like to buy it and to live there."

"Oh how magnificent!" exclaimed Malcolm very dramatically. Then opening the top drawer of a tall filing cabinet in the corner of the room, he took out some papers.

Clive had been brought up by his parents to be very honest, and he was now quite worried that he had gone into the castle without permission, had a lovely sleep there and a lovely bath, and some supper.

"Malcolm, I feel I must be perfectly honest about something," said Clive.

"And what might that be?" asked Malcolm.

"Well," began Clive, "when I discovered the castle I was feeling rather tired. I rang the bell twice, and when there was no answer I crept in as the door was open a little bit. I had a look around, I ran myself a lovely bubble bath, I had something to eat, and a most wonderful sleep in that oh so cosy bed. I feel I must pay for my stay."

Malcolm thought for a moment, then he spoke. "I think, Clive, that you are actually a very nice chap, and thank you for being so honest. You do not have to pay for your stay. I am extremely happy to think that I will have such a nice neighbour."

Clive beamed. What a very happy crocodile he was! His parents would be proud of him! Malcolm put the papers from the filing cabinet in front of Clive, and with a great wave of his beautiful wing, he gave Clive a pen made from one of his very own feathers. He showed Clive where to sign his name, so that the castle would then belong to him.

So that is how Clive came to live in the castle. He was quite content living all by himself and loved knitting. In fact, he had knitted all the curtains for his castle, in pink wool. Having found there were no lights in the castle, Clive soon discovered lots of candles in a kitchen cupboard. Clive would sit up long into the night knitting away by candle light. Sometimes, though, when he'd had enough of knitting, he would long for some company. Malcolm had popped in twice for a cup of tea, but Clive would often look out to sea from his castle windows, wondering if anything exciting would ever happen.

CHAPTER 5

On the other side of ocean, Great Grandma and Mincemeat were making their way down the river bank, pulling the Magic Raspberry with them as they went. Great Grandma stepped inside and settled herself on the cosy rug that Mincemeat had put there earlier. He started up the engine and the Magic Raspberry slipped down the river bank out into the water.

They sailed all that day and all that night. When it grew dark, Mincemeat carefully lit the pumpkin lanterns that hung all around the Magic

Raspberry. Warm light flooded inside where Great Grandma was sitting. She felt very cosy, and thought it was time for supper. She unwrapped one of the meat and potato pies and called Mincemeat. He pressed the 'Float' button, and the engine went quiet. Great Grandma cut a piece each for them from one of the huge pies, and they had a lovely

supper. Carefully wrapping the pie up again, she put it back in the suitcase. They finished off their supper with a dead fly biscuit each and a glass of blackberry squash, and both settled down under the very snugly yellow spotted rug to sleep.

The Magic Raspberry floated all night long. Great Grandma and Mincemeat slept soundly. When the sun rose the next morning they were in the middle of the ocean. After a lovely breakfast of fried dandelions and parsnip juice, Mincemeat started up the engine.

Sailing along, Great Grandma fell asleep. All of a sudden there was a huge sign in the water. It said 'South China Sea'.

Mincemeat shrieked out with excitement "Great Grandma, Great Grandma, we're in the South China Sea!"

Great Grandma awoke with a start. "Oh my goodness," she exclaimed "the South China Sea!"

"Yes!" said Mincemeat.

Just at that very minute, there was a loud clonking sound from the engine, and the engine completely stopped. A big flashing sign came up next to the steering wheel, 'Fish Finger and Chip Alert! Fish Finger and Chip

Alert!' and a siren started 'Nee Naw! Nee Naw! Nee Naw!' *Oh galloping grasshoppers,* thought Mincemeat, *I had better have a look at the engine!* He opened up a hatch by the steering wheel and crawled in. There was the trouble! One of the largest fish fingers and two of the chips had come loose from the wheel cogs. They were rusty. *Oh no,* Mincemeat said to himself, *I forgot to oil the engine!* Whilst all this was happening, Great Grandma had fallen asleep again, for she was very tired from the adventure. Mincemeat could see that they were floating nearer and nearer to an island!

As you know, Clive the Crocodile loved racing cars! He was out in the sunshine going round and round his race track in his bright blue sports car, driving faster and faster. He was having such a wonderful time that he did not hear the cries for help from the Magic Raspberry. Finally he decided to put his car away in the garage, and that is when he heard Mincemeat calling, for they were now quite close to the island.

But the first thing that Clive heard was the siren from the Magic Raspberry. *Whatever is that noise?* he thought to himself.

There was Mincemeat frantically waving "Over here, over here!" he called. "We've conked out! Please can you help?!"

Clive ran down the shore and sprang into the water. Swimming as fast as he could over to the Magic Raspberry, he then pushed the Magic Raspberry with all his might over to the shore. He wedged it with lots and lots of seaweed so that it wouldn't float away.

By this time, Great Grandma had woken up from all the commotion. "Good heavens!" she exclaimed. "Whatever is going on?"

Mincemeat told her all about the trouble with the engine, ".....but we've been rescued!" he said.

Clive bobbed up from the water so that he could look inside the Magic Raspberry. "Hello, I'm Clive," he announced smiling.

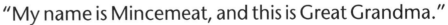

"Oh thank you so much for rescuing us" said Mincemeat. "My name is Mincemeat, and this is Great Grandma."

Taking hold of Great Grandma's hand, for Clive was a real gentleman, he said, "I am delighted to meet you my dear, my name is Clive, the proud owner of this very grand castle you can see behind you. Please step ashore, and come inside. I think that you may need a good rest after all your adventures and some refreshments perhaps?"

"How very kind of you," said Great Grandma, as she stepped out of the Magic Raspberry with Clive's help, followed by Mincemeat, and they all walked up the path to the castle. Inside, Clive invited them to sit and relax in the lounge.

"Oh, what a cosy room!" said Great Grandma, and she and Mincemeat both snuggled themselves on the sofa.

Clive excused himself and went into the kitchen. There, he prepared a wonderful snack of fresh turnip juice and squashed tomatoes on toast. Putting it all on a tray, he carried it into the lounge. "How lovely," said Great Grandma. "I love squashed tomatoes! I was just admiring your curtains, did you make them yourself?" she enquired.

"Indeed I did" said Clive proudly, "I absolutely love knitting."

When everyone was nicely full from the tasty snack Clive had made, Great Grandma fell sound asleep on the sofa. Clive and Mincemeat crept out of the lounge and into the kitchen, and Mincemeat helped Clive wash everything up.

"Now," said Clive, when they had finished, "let's have a look at this engine trouble of yours."

It just so happens that Clive was a bit of a wizard at mending engines! And a jolly good job too, because it wasn't just the loose fish finger and chips that was the trouble. Clive found some old dried up peas rolling about the engine that had stopped the wheel cogs from moving round properly. Mincemeat was a real help, passing Clive the spanners and the engine manual, so that Clive could read what to do next. Soon he had it fixed, asking Mincemeat to step inside and start up the Magic Raspberry. The engine sprang to life, and Clive stood there very proudly, very pleased with his work.

"Hooray, hooray," Clive said, "I think it is time for tea."

So they all had tea on Great Grandma's best china tea set that Mincemeat had packed so carefully before they had left.

CHAPTER 6

Mincemeat and Great Grandma were so grateful to Clive for fixing the Magic Raspberry that they wished to repay him in some way. Mincemeat loved baking, and Clive loved currant scones. So it was decided that Mincemeat would bake Clive a huge batch of currant scones. Very luckily, Mincemeat had packed his 'I Love Cooking' apron! *Well if you go on an adventure, you never know what you might need,* Mincemeat had thought to himself.

Soon enough, the whole castle was filled with the most delicious smell of freshly baked scones. Clive had given Mincemeat a sack of currants, and every single one went into the baking. Clive telephoned Malcolm, and asked him to join them for tea.

Malcolm said he would be "positively delighted!"

Great Grandma and Mincemeat were really very tired from their adventure, and so Clive kindly asked them to stay the night. Clive gave Great

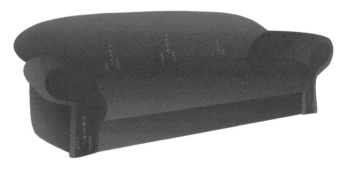

Grandma his 'oh so cosy' bed with the huge white duvet made from the softest feathers in the world. Clive and Mincemeat snuggled down for the night in the lounge. Clive stretched out on the sofa, and Mincemeat

curled up into a ball in one of the comfy red armchairs by the fireplace.

The next morning after a lovely breakfast of seaweed burgers, Great Grandma felt that she had had enough of adventuring for the time being, and that she would like to return home. Because Mincemeat always looked after her so beautifully and with so much love, he said he would happily set sail for home. Clive said that they must keep in touch, and gave Great Grandma his telephone number. Great Grandma and Mincemeat had enjoyed such a lovely stay with Clive, and she promised to ring him as soon as they returned home. She insisted Clive must come and stay with them very soon.

The sun was setting in the sky as Clive waved Great Grandma and Mincemeat off from the shore. The sky was the most beautiful shade of

pinks and reds and oranges, as the sun sank lower and lower. The Magic Raspberry was soon disappearing from view. Clive watched as it got smaller and smaller as it sailed into the distance, soon becoming a little dot on the horizon.

CHAPTER 7

Winter was setting in on the island. The evenings were getting quite chilly now. Clive went back inside the castle after watching the Magic Raspberry sail away, and, taking a big pile of logs, he lit a roaring log fire. He settled into one of the comfy red armchairs by the side of the fire, putting a cosy pink rug that, of course, he had knitted himself, over his knees. Soon he fell fast asleep, and was dreaming of the wonderful visit he had had from Great Grandma and Mincemeat.

Far far away on the other side of the ocean, the Magic Raspberry sailed towards the river bank at the bottom of the cottage garden. Great Grandma and Mincemeat were safely back.

"What a wonderful adventure we have had," Great Grandma said to Mincemeat as she took the front door key from under the flowerpot and unlocked the front door, "but it's good to be home."

Mincemeat agreed.

GREAT GRANDMA AND THE RUNAWAY TRAIN

CHAPTER 1

The notice at Jelly Junction station was written in bold letters. It said:

Mr Gerald Jeremiah Horatio Golightly
Station Master
Jelly Junction

Mr Golightly had a huge moustache and very twinkly brown eyes, and he was very very smiley. Mr Golightly was the kindest man in all the world.

As well as being the Station Master, he was also the ticket inspector on the train, and he loved calling out "Tickets please, tickets please," as he passed through the carriages.

Theo lived in the train shed at Jelly Junction. He was a very handsome train. Theo's engine was painted in black shiny paint, and he had lots of carriages painted red, which matched his huge red wheels. The seats inside Theo were made of wood.

Theo was a very happy train, but he longed for an adventure. Stanley Butterfingers was the train driver.

Great Grandma and Mincemeat were going to visit Great Grandma's Aunt Petunia, who lived in the countryside at

Fieldmouse Meadows. They were getting on the train at Muddleford. It was called Muddleford because everything at the station was so muddled up and upside down! To begin with, the ticket office was on the roof of the station, and you had to go up a ladder to buy your

ticket! The waiting room was outside the station in the bus stop, instead of on the station platform! The big clock always showed the wrong time, and when it got to twelve o'clock, the hands of the clock whizzed round and round so fast that nobody could tell the time at all!

Stanley Butterfingers loved driving Theo all about the countryside. Even when Stanley had a day off, he would spend it with Theo in the train shed polishing him, and Theo would sigh a happy contented sigh. Theo loved carrying all the passengers to all the stations along the route.

But Theo longed for an adventure.

Mincemeat had been very busy for the last few days organizing a scrumptious picnic to take on the train. He had done some more baking. Mincemeat always wore his 'I Love Cooking' apron whenever he was busy in the kitchen cooking. In fact, he had tried out a new recipe that he had made up himself only yesterday. It was geranium and acorn bread, and Mincemeat had collected the acorns from the big old oak tree at the bottom of the hill. He had also made a conker cake from an old recipe given to him by his own grandma, and Mincemeat had collected the conkers for his cake from the horse chestnut tree in the cottage garden. Also for the picnic, Mincemeat had made fried dandelion and nettle sandwiches, made with the geranium and acorn bread. Then he put everything needed for the picnic in a wicker basket, with some cheese flavoured chocolate especially for Great Grandma, and finally a bottle of cherryade.

The train was leaving Jelly Junction at exactly ten o'clock. The first stop was Muddleford. Mincemeat put the wicker basket in the rack on the back of his motorbike, and helping Great Grandma climb into the sidecar, he gave Great Grandma her crash helmet. He then put on his own, together with his black spotted motorbike rider's suit. Jumping on to the driver's seat, and hanging Great Grandma's handbag from his tail, Mincemeat started up the engine.

When they got to Muddleford station, Mincemeat parked his motorbike on the station platform in the bicycle rack. The train was due to arrive at Muddleford at exactly half past ten. First of all, they had to buy their tickets. Mincemeat found

a nice seat for Great Grandma in the waiting room in the bus stop, whilst he went to buy the tickets. He climbed the ladder up to the ticket office and asked for "Two tickets to Fieldmouse Meadows please," which was the last stop on the track.

CHAPTER 2

Jelly Junction at half past nine in the morning was a very busy station indeed. Lots of people were bustling this way and that, buying tickets, stopping to buy the Jelly Junction Times which was sold at the newspaper stand, and passengers were running down the platform to get on board the train. Mr Gerald Jeremiah Horatio Golightly, Station Master at Jelly Junction, blew his whistle loudly.

"Everybody on board now please! Everybody on board!" he shouted, and he blew his whistle again even louder this time.

Then climbing on board into the driver's cab next to Stanley, and leaning out of the window to look down the platform, he made sure that all the train doors were shut. Stanley started up the engine, and slowly Theo moved along the platform and out of the station along the railway track. Theo's engine was made from old bicycle tyres and wooden spoons, and made a bit of a clonking sound as he passed up the track. The faster he went, the louder he clonked, but all the passengers were quite used to the funny noises Theo made.

Theo arrived at Muddleford at half past ten on the dot. People got out of the train and people got on. Helping Great Grandma onto the train, Mincemeat

climbed on board himself. They found lovely seats by the window, for Great Grandma loved to look out and see the countryside as they travelled along. Mr Golightly walked up and down the platform making sure all the doors were closed, and blew his whistle. Then he jumped on board next to Stanley.

Theo chugged through the countryside. It was a beautiful day, and they passed fields and farms. There were cows in one field, sheep in the field next to them, and horses in another. Further along the journey, the farmer was out in his red tractor gathering in all the hay for the animals for the winter months. They would come in from the fields when it was too cold to stay outside, and live cosily in the barns munching on the hay.

The next station was Daffodil Hill. Everywhere you looked were hundreds and hundreds of yellow daffodils. They were in hanging baskets at the station, and in the fields all around the station were rows and rows of daffodils. Even the ticket office was covered in yellow daffodils. There was

even a flower stand on the platform selling daffodils! Mincemeat had never seen anything like it.

All of a sudden he had an idea! He wanted to buy a bunch of daffodils for Great Grandma for he knew she loved flowers! He leapt up from his seat and off the train before Great Grandma had a chance to say 'jumping jackdaws' or to ask him what he was doing. Running over to the flower stall, Mincemeat picked up the biggest bunch he could find, and paid the money.

Mr Golightly had not seen Mincemeat leap from the train, and, as all the doors were shut, he blew his whistle and Theo moved along the platform pulling out of the station. At that minute, Mincemeat turned round to get back on the train!

Great Grandma was jumping up and down and banging on the window "Mincemeat, Mincemeat!" she cried.

Mr Golightly and Stanley had not noticed that Mincemeat was now running faster and faster along the platform holding his bunch of flowers!

"Wait for me, wait for me!" he shouted loudly, and he ran as hard as he could!

Just as the last carriage of the train was coming to the end of the platform leaving the station, Mr Golightly thought he heard shouting! "Put the brakes on Stanley! I can hear shouting!"

By this time, Mincemeat was standing on the platform bent over and gasping for breath. His lovely ginger fur had fluffed out even more with all the effort of running up the platform. Stanley put his foot hard on the brakes, and the train came to a stop with a screeching sound. Mr Golightly walked back through the carriages and, getting off the train, he went over to Mincemeat and put his arm round him.

Mincemeat took a few moments to catch his breath. Then he said "Oh, I am so sorry Mr Golightly, I never meant to cause all this upset, it's just that I so much wanted to buy a bunch of those beautiful daffodils for Great Grandma." The daffodils by this time were looking rather sad and floppy.

Because he was the kindest man in all the world, Mr Golightly said, "Now don't you worry, Mincemeat. You were being kind and thoughtful, and wanted to make Great Grandma happy. You sit here for a moment on this bench, whilst I go into the ticket office and get you a glass of water."

A minute later, Mr Golightly came back with the water and Mincemeat drank it thirstily. "Now, which carriage were you sitting in?"

"Carriage number two, I think" Mincemeat said.

"Stanley, reverse the train please, we need carriage number two," shouted Mr Golightly.

Stanley put the big gear lever into reverse, and Theo slowly moved backwards down the platform. Mr Golightly helped Mincemeat up and into the carriage. Great Grandma was still standing by the window.

"Now then Great Grandma, don't you be cross with him, Mincemeat was just trying to make you happy by buying you a bunch of flowers."

"Oh I couldn't be cross with Mincemeat, he's far too lovely for that," she said. She put her arms round him, and taking the sad looking daffodils from him she said, "Thank you Mincemeat, it was a lovely thought. You sit down and enjoy the rest of the journey, I am just glad that you are safe."

Mr Golightly got off the train and, walking up the platform, he climbed into the driver's cab next to Stanley.

CHAPTER 3

Mr Golightly, passing through the carriages, called "Tickets please, tickets please, next station is Bumblebee Bridge, Bumblebee Bridge next station."

Those passengers who would be getting off began gathering their belongings together.

Mincemeat had fallen asleep after his adventure of nearly missing the train, and he woke up feeling rather hungry, so he and Great Grandma decided to have their picnic.

The train journey took them part of the way along the coast, and Theo travelled along the track high above the sea. The views were wonderful, they could see a boat coming into the harbour at Ice Cream Cove. The picnic lasted until they came slowly into the station at Ice Cream Cove. There, a whole family of seagulls got into the carriage where Great Grandma and Mincemeat were sitting. Chatting noisily, they tried to decide where to sit, and some of the little ones were pushing and shoving each other. Then, one of the baby seagulls spotted the

remains of the picnic. Without asking, he snatched the last piece of conker cake and gobbled it up.

His mother was cross! "Cecil," she said, "you naughty boy. You don't just help yourself to other people's food, and especially without asking. It's too late now, you've eaten it, but you apologize now to the nice lady and her lovely cat."

Cecil hung his head. "I'm sorry," he said very quietly.

"Good boy," said his mother. "Now, all of you come and sit down nicely, and no pushing and shoving, and no squawking" she said to her six children.

They all did as they were told, and sat in a row looking out of the window until they got to the next station which was Baked Bean Bay, where they all got off and waddled off down the platform.

As Theo was coming back down the track away from the sea, he fancied his adventure should begin! Stanley was steering him as usual. All of a sudden, Theo put on a spurt and started speeding along! He sped along under bridges, whizzing past fields, and he was going so fast that he was making the trees along the side of the track blow about. Stanley couldn't stop him, and Theo was having so much fun he was laughing! Everyone on the train couldn't believe what was happening, as the countryside shot past the windows for they were going so fast!

Great Grandma thought it was wonderful! "Oh how exciting!" she exclaimed.

Mincemeat's fur was blowing flat against his gorgeous ginger face from the wind coming in through the open window! Stanley was trying to slow Theo down. But Theo was having far too much fun for that! He went faster and faster! He sped past a lake. The swans on the lake stopped and stared at the runaway train for they couldn't believe their eyes! The next station coming up was Hamster Heights and Theo was meant to stop there.

Mr Golightly spoke on the loudspeaker "Next station Hamster Heights, Hamster Heights next station. Theo, will you please slow down at once!"

But Theo didn't! He hurtled right through the station!

On and on he flew, laughing all the way. People had heard about the runaway train, and they were coming out of their houses and onto the bridges above the railway track to have a look. Farmers stopped what they were doing and ran to the edge of their fields to have a look. Bert, the village policeman from the nearby village of Toffee Apple Green, was waiting with his bicycle to go over the railway crossing safely. He was standing by the barrier when Theo thundered through. He must have been going 100 miles an hour!

"Dancing dormice!" he exclaimed, "Whatever is going on?"

Bert knew Theo well and often waved to Stanley from the bridge above the railway track, as Stanley drove the train. Great Grandma still thought it was all very exciting! Mincemeat was not so sure.

Theo thought it was very funny and was laughing harder than ever!

"Whatever are we to do Mr Golightly?" asked Stanley.

Mr Golightly, who was usually very smiley, now looked quite serious, and twirling his big moustache round and round his fingers, he thought just how to slow Theo down.

"There is only one thing for it Stanley," said Mr Golightly. "I will have to pull the emergency cord," and that is just what he did.

The next station was Duckling Down, and as Mr Golightly could see the station approaching, he pulled hard on the emergency cord. Theo's wheels made the hugest screeching sound as the train came to a stop alongside the platform.

CHAPTER 4

Theo, by this time, was quite out of breath and he knew he was in trouble. Stanley and Mr Golightly both got down from the driver's cab.

"What do you think you were doing?" said Stanley to Theo crossly. "My passengers have missed their stop at Hamster Heights!"

Theo was panting, trying to catch his breath.

"Well" said Stanley, "what have you got to say for yourself?"

Theo coughed, and said in a very deep voice and rather sadly, "All I wanted was a bit of an adventure."

"Well, you have certainly had that," said Mr Golightly. "If you were bored Theo, you should have told Stanley, and you could have talked about it. Maybe we could have changed the route to make it more interesting for you. I am sure we could have sorted something out."

"I'm sorry," Theo said slowly. "I never meant to cause trouble, honestly I didn't."

Mr Golightly could see that Theo was truly sorry, because big tear drops welled up in his eyes. Mr Golightly, being so kind, got out his big white handkerchief from his waistcoat pocket and dried Theo's eyes.

"There there," he said to Theo. "Don't cry, but if you ever have a problem or you feel unhappy please remember, always come to Stanley or to me and I promise you we can sort it out."

After such an adventure, Theo was quite tired, so he had a rest at Duckling Down before they continued the journey. He needed a lot of water in his engine after all that speeding along. All the passengers settled back down, but everyone on the train was talking about it. Passing through the carriages checking the tickets, Mr Golightly apologized to those passengers who had missed their stop at Hamster Heights. None of them actually seemed to mind too much, and said they had really enjoyed the adventure!

The next stop was Marshmallow Ridge. The ticket office at Marshmallow Ridge was made of pink and white marshmallows! The benches on the station platform were soft and springy because they were made of marshmallows too!

There was even a sweet shop on the platform that sold nothing but marshmallows! Mincemeat was just thinking to himself how he would love a bag of marshmallows. He'd had quite enough for one day though, when he nearly missed the train buying the daffodils! Then a little boy got on the train with his mother, and sat next to Mincemeat. The little boy was clutching a paper bag full to the top with marshmallows. He stretched out his arm and offered the bag to Mincemeat.

"Thank you," said Mincemeat. "That is so kind of you." Mincemeat chose a pink one, and beamed at the little boy.

Theo chugged along through the open countryside until they reached Sweetcorn Central.

Mr Golightly announced the station. "Next station Sweetcorn Central, Sweetcorn Central next station."

Not many passengers got on at Sweetcorn Central as the next station was Fieldmouse Meadows, and the last stop on the line. Mincemeat settled down to read his cookery book, and Great Grandma fell fast asleep.

CHAPTER 5

Theo was feeling very tired after all the excitement of racing through the countryside, and he pulled in alongside Fieldmouse Meadows station platform slowly. Mr Golightly decided that as Theo was so weary, he should spend the night there in the train shed for a good night's rest, and go back to Jelly Junction the next morning.

Mr Golightly spoke on the loudspeaker "Last stop now, Fieldmouse Meadows, Fieldmouse Meadows last stop. Please make sure you all have your belongings with you. Thank you very much for travelling with Golightly Railways. I hope you have enjoyed your journey, and I hope you will travel with us again very soon."

Great Grandma woke up as Theo came to a stop with a little jolt. Mincemeat put his cookery book away in the wicker basket. It was his very best cookery book and he didn't want to lose it! Clutching the basket, he helped Great Grandma down from the train.

Aunt Petunia was waiting in her beautiful car outside the station to meet them. The car was made from an old pumpkin. Great Grandma got in beside Aunt Petunia, and

Mincemeat sat with the wicker basket on his knees. They rattled along country lanes, Great Grandma and Aunt Petunia chatting away, with Mincemeat enjoying the scenery.

Soon, they got to Aunt Petunia's cottage in Lupin Lane. They all went inside, and Aunt Petunia made a nice pot of tea. Mincemeat lifted out a red checked cloth from the wicker basket. Inside were the sage and lavender scones he had made freshly that morning for Aunt Petunia, and he put them on the tray. They had tea in the garden as it was such a lovely sunny day.

"Now then," said Aunt Petunia. "Do you have any interesting news?"

"Oh, indeed we have!" said Great Grandma, and she and Mincemeat proceeded to tell her all about the adventure with Theo the runaway train, and Mincemeat's adventure with the daffodils.

"My goodness me," said Aunt Petunia. "What an exciting day!"

They all agreed it had been a most exciting day!

Garden
Sage

GREAT GRANDMA GOES UNDER THE SEA

CHAPTER 1

One day, a letter plopped through the letter box of Great Grandma's cottage. Mincemeat, Great Grandma's extremely lovely large ginger cat, was busy in the kitchen making bluebell bread. As you know, he loved baking and always wore his 'I Love Cooking' apron. He had picked the bluebells from the garden himself that morning. Trotting out to the hall, he picked up the letter from the front door mat and took it out to Great Grandma who was gardening. Taking off her gardening gloves, she opened the letter. It was an invitation.

Dear Great Grandma and Mincemeat, the invitation began, **we are having a gathering next Friday at 4 o'clock, and would love it if you could come and stay for a few days. The address for the gathering is: Oyster Shell Cottage, Fish Pie Lane, Under The Sea. Cousin Cyril Crab owns Turtle Towers, a lovely little hotel, and he would be delighted to accommodate you. Please let us know. With love from your cousins, Ogilvie Octopus and Pearl Oyster.**

"Well," said Great Grandma to Mincemeat. "What a nice surprise. It's quite a while since we have been anywhere, and we haven't seen our cousins for a very long time. Wouldn't it be exciting! We must telephone immediately! Of course, we would have to spring clean the submarine, Mincemeat."

"Oh no problem there Great Grandma," Mincemeat said eagerly. "In fact I was just thinking to myself the other day that it could do with a new coat of paint. What colour would you like it painted Great Grandma?"

Great Grandma thought for a moment, and said, "You know Mincemeat, I think I may fancy bright pink!"

So bright pink it was to be then!

Mincemeat went back inside the cottage, and telephoning the cousins, he

 said, "Great Grandma and I would both love to come to the gathering and to stay at Turtle Towers."

He then checked on the bluebell bread baking in the oven. *Five more minutes* he said to himself, sniffing the wonderful aroma of the freshly baking bread. He washed up all the cooking utensils whilst he was waiting. Five minutes later, putting on his oven gloves, he very carefully took the bread out of the oven. Then he went back outside to the garden where Great Grandma, at the bottom of the garden, was planting a row of dandelions, for she loved dandelion salad!

"I'm just going to get the paint!" he called, and with that he jumped on his motor bike. Putting on his safety helmet and black spotted motor bike rider's suit, he drove carefully down the hill. Revving the engine, he sped off along the lane.

Upon his return, Mincemeat unloaded the tins of paint from the rack on the back of his motor bike, and put them in the garden shed where the submarine lived. The next morning bright and early, Mincemeat went out to the shed and set to work to paint the submarine. Firstly, he put on his painting overalls, for he did not want to get paint on his beautiful ginger fur. Putting on the radio, he began singing along to the music whilst he worked, for he loved singing. To begin with, he rubbed all the old paint off the submarine which had started to go rusty and brown. It was such a long time since Great Grandma and Mincemeat had used it. Then he set to. *I think this will need five coats of paint,* Mincemeat thought to himself. We shall need it nice and water tight.

Two hours later, Mincemeat stood back and admired his work. The first two coats were dry, and he thought it time to stop for a nice cup of tea. He went inside the cottage, and soon came out with two lovely steaming mugs and a plate of dead fly biscuits for them both to share. Great Grandma was still busy, planting a whole vegetable patch of parsnips, carrots, and turnips. She was just picking a large bunch of stinging nettles to make a lovely soup as Mincemeat came out with the tray. Together they sat on the hammock and had their tea and biscuits.

CHAPTER 2

Three days later, Mincemeat had finished all the painting. The submarine looked positively splendid! Mincemeat was so proud. There it stood in the shed all bright and shiny and very very pink! Great Grandma came out to the shed to see the submarine. She stood back and admired it.

"Well, Mincemeat," she said, "you have certainly made a wonderful job of that!" Then she kissed his lovely furry face.

Mincemeat thought it wise to check that the engine of the submarine was in perfect working order. The engine was made of liquorice. Taking every strand out, and having oiled them all, Mincemeat then put everything back together again. Next, he made sure that the hatch on the roof where they would climb in, was quite water tight. They didn't want any leaks! After that, Mincemeat tested the dials, for they showed how deep the submarine was going. Finally he tested the hooter, for the sea could be a very busy place, and he might need to honk the horn a lot!

It seemed that everything was in order.

Great Grandma wanted to take presents to their cousins, which was the right thing to do of course. She wanted to take one for Ogilvie Octopus and one for Pearl Oyster. She also wanted to take a present for Cyril Crab. When

Mincemeat had spoken to him on the telephone, he had insisted that Great Grandma and Mincemeat did not pay for their stay at Turtle Towers.

Great Grandma thought that Ogilvie may appreciate a book on fishing, and for Pearl, she had a beautiful necklace made of tiny blue and pink seashells that had belonged to Great Grandma's aunty. For Cyril, she would take a painting set as she remembered that he loved painting pictures, and she was sure she may see some of his work decorating the walls of his hotel, Turtle Towers.

The very next day, Great Grandma and Mincemeat set out on their trip to see their cousins.

The submarine had lovely thick yellow carpet and two very comfy pink armchairs. Great Grandma and Mincemeat climbed up the ladder on the side of

the submarine and through the open hatch. Once inside, Mincemeat closed the hatch, and they settled themselves in. Driving the submarine to the water's edge of the river bank, Mincemeat pressed the 'Splash' button and the submarine lifted up and plopped right into the water. Next, Mincemeat pressed the 'Plonk' button and they started to go down and down into the water. The deeper they went, the darker it got, so Mincemeat put on the headlights. Bright light streamed through the water and they saw the most wonderful things out of the windows. There were the most beautiful fish. Some were dark blue with

orange stripes, some were light blue and yellow, and some were orange with white stripes! Hundreds of brightly coloured anemones in orange and yellow,

grew on large rocks and rocked backwards and forwards as the submarine passed by. Mincemeat put on the windscreen wipers to help him see where they were going. All of a sudden two turtles appeared and were smiling and waving to them! Great Grandma and Mincemeat waved back excitedly. Then an extremely tickly octopus swam past with all his

arms and legs moving very gently through the water, and quickly disappeared into a huge shell. *It must be very tiring to have all those arms and legs, he's probably going to have a sleep,* thought Mincemeat.

The dials on the submarine showed that they were going very deep indeed. Mincemeat set the dial to 'Seabed'. The engine made a roaring sound and down and down they went. Quite suddenly and with a little jolt, they felt the submarine land on the sandy seabed, and there in front of them was a sign directing them to the hotel where they were going to stay, **Turtle Towers**. Mincemeat drove the submarine along the seabed until there was a big door in the rocks, and a beautiful mermaid

waiting there. The mermaid took a key from behind the rocks, and opened the door. It was large enough for the submarine to go through, and Mincemeat carefully steered the submarine through to the other side. The mermaid followed them and closed the door.

On the other side of the door, there was no water.

There were crabs scuttling about, and lobsters lazily stretched out on rocks munching seaweed. There was a group of oysters chatting noisily together and laughing at a fish joke! There were two turtles deep in conversation and looking very serious. One kept nodding in agreement it seemed, with what his friend was saying.

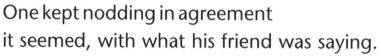

The mermaid was waiting to welcome Great Grandma and Mincemeat. Mincemeat pressed the 'Park' button, and opened the hatch of the submarine. The mermaid helped Great Grandma down the ladder, with Mincemeat following carrying the luggage.

"Good morning," the mermaid said. "My name is Milly, and we are all so happy to see you both."

Everybody crowded round, chatting excitedly, for they all wanted to meet Great Grandma and Mincemeat, and had been talking about the visit the whole week!

CHAPTER 3

"You must be quite tired after your journey," said Milly. "I will show you to your hotel."

Great Grandma and Mincemeat followed Milly. They walked down a wiggly path made of very flat sea shells. There in a clearing stood the most beautiful hotel they had ever seen. It was a huge tall shell decorated with blue flowers. The curtains in the windows were made of seaweed! Standing in the doorway was cousin Cyril Crab. He was dressed very smartly in matching black and white checked trousers and jacket, and a checked hat.

"Good morning my dears," said Cyril, in a very deep voice. "I am so happy to welcome you both to Turtle Towers."

Inside the hotel, the armchairs were made from old turtle shells turned the other way up and had soft green cushions on the seats. The beds were made from huge oyster shells and had snugly white duvets and soft white pillows on them.

After having a little rest, Great Grandma and Mincemeat went to explore outside. They came across a lovely cave in which there was a school. Cousin Pearl was a school teacher. She was a plump and very jolly oyster. Seeing

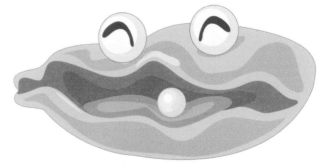

Great Grandma and Mincemeat standing in the doorway of the cave, Pearl invited them in to the classroom, whilst she finished the lessons for the day. Pearl was doing some times tables with the children. The children in the class were shrimps, small crabs, limpets and mussels, and there were all sorts of small fish too.

Lionel the Limpet was always falling asleep in the lessons! This time he was snoring!!

"Whoever is making that noise?!" said Pearl.

All the children started giggling! Pearl had to stop herself from laughing too! Lionel carried on snoring. Then Pearl realized where the noise was coming from. She walked over to where Lionel was, and tapped him on his shell. Lionel awoke with a start and for a minute didn't know where he was.

"Lionel, you've been sleeping again!" said Pearl. "I am going to have to write a letter for you to take home to your mother, saying that you need to go to bed earlier. Why are you so tired?"

"I've been watching a fishing programme on television Miss," said Lionel brightly. "It was ever so interesting, it was all about............"

"I am really not interested in what it was about Lionel, now sit up straight and pay attention," said Pearl.

The children started reciting their times tables:

"Two twos are four shrimps"

"Two threes are six sardines"

"Two fours are eight sprats"

"Very well done, children," said Pearl. "Please will you ring the bell for the end of school," she asked Sidney, who was the tallest shrimp in the class. "Now everybody, please line up by the door and wait nicely for your parents to collect you."

CHAPTER 4

The next day was the day of the gathering at Oyster Shell Cottage. There was plenty to do to get everything organized. Great Grandma and Mincemeat wanted to help.

First there was the shopping to do. Mincemeat said he would be very happy to do the shopping. Milly said she would take him in her car, which was made out of old fish bones. Milly's friend, Jeremy Jellyfish had a shop, and he had everything in his shop that they could possibly need for the gathering. Milly drove Mincemeat there. They bought lemonade and crisps, and lots and lots of fish flavoured chocolate! Milly thought it would be a good idea to buy cherry and marmalade pies, seaweed cakes, strawberry buns, and crunchy sand biscuits! Mincemeat said he rather fancied the fish food muffins, so those went in the shopping trolley too. The shopping trolleys were old sea shells on wheels. Finally they chose a red tablecloth with serviettes to match.

Milly, driving them back, turned into Fish Pie Lane and parked outside Oyster Shell Cottage. Mincemeat and Milly unloaded the shopping from the car and took it inside. There, they laid the table with the red tablecloth and all the goodies. What a treat it looked!

At four o'clock everybody started arriving. Ogilvie Octopus welcomed all the guests, as it was his cottage. So many friends came! There were herrings and mackerels, sardines and sprats, shrimps and jellyfish, crabs and lobsters, limpets and sea urchins, oysters and turtles, and a whole family of mussels. Everybody crowded into the cottage. It was ever so noisy with everyone talking at the same time it seemed! But they had a wonderful time and loved the food! Great Grandma said that they had never been to such a lovely gathering, and Mincemeat had made lots of new friends.

Soon it was time for everybody to go home. But somebody was missing! Montgomery, one of the mussels was nowhere to be seen. Everybody started looking. They searched all around the cottage, but couldn't find him. Then they searched the school, but still couldn't find him. All this time no-one had noticed that Lionel was missing too! Lionel and Montgomery were very best friends. Sidney Shrimp said he would go to Jeremy's shop to see if Montgomery had gone to buy sweets, but when he got there Jeremy said he hadn't seen him either. Everyone was getting worried.

But still no-one had noticed that Lionel was missing too!

CHAPTER 5

There was a new arrival at Turtle Towers. Sapphire the Sea Horse had come for a week's holiday. She was an elderly sea horse. She always walked with a walking stick these days, and she was feeling very tired. Cyril Crab was helping Sapphire in with her luggage.

"I have a lovely room at the back of the hotel for you overlooking the garden, and it is on the ground floor so you won't have to go up any stairs," said Cyril. "It will be nice and quiet and you can have a jolly good rest."

"Oh, that is perfect," said Sapphire. "Just what I need, thank you so much."

"My pleasure," said Cyril.

"I think I would just like to sit for a little rest first in the garden if I may," said Sapphire.

"Of course, my dear," said Cyril, showing her to one of the comfy rocking chairs. "In fact, why don't you have your supper out here, it is such a lovely evening," suggested Cyril.

"What a good idea," said Sapphire. So she ordered a delicious supper of seaweed soup and pink jelly.

At that moment, Great Grandma and Mincemeat, who were also staying at Turtle Towers of course, came out into the garden.

"What a delightful garden," said Great Grandma. "Would you mind if we sat with you?"

"That would be lovely," said Sapphire. "In fact, why don't you join me for supper?"

"That's very kind of you," said Great Grandma, "we would love to, wouldn't we Mincemeat?"

Mincemeat beamed, and they all introduced themselves to each other.

After supper, Sapphire said goodnight to Great Grandma and Mincemeat, and Cyril showed Sapphire to her room. The bed was huge! Sapphire had never seen such a snugly duvet in all her life! She pottered about the bedroom, unpacking all her things. She was very particular about hanging all her dresses up in a neat row, and put all the matching shoes and handbags with the right dresses. Then she put her pearl necklace and pearl earrings on the dressing table with her hair brush. Next she put all her bits and bobs in the bathroom. By this time she was feeling quite tired, and so she settled down in one of the armchairs. She put on the television. *Oh not another programme on fishing,* she thought. *I am rather fed up with those!* She must have then dozed off, because when she woke up the room was in darkness. Sapphire reached out to the little table by the armchair and switched on the shell lamp. A lovely glow filled the room.

CHAPTER 6

At first, Sapphire couldn't make out where the noise was coming from. She was sure she could hear snoring! She got up out of the armchair and began looking all around the room. She looked in the wardrobe, she looked behind the curtains, she looked under the dressing table, she looked in the bathroom, and then she looked in the bed! There, fast fast asleep snuggled up together were Montgomery and Lionel.

"Oh jumping jellyfish!" Sapphire exclaimed out loud. "Whatever are you two doing here?!"

Lionel and Montgomery woke up with a start. They told Sapphire that they had wandered away from the gathering for a little adventure.

"Don't you know that was a very silly thing to do, and wasn't safe at all," scolded Sapphire. "You could have got very lost. Both of you wait here whilst I tell the gentleman who owns the hotel that you are here with me."

Sapphire went to find Cyril, and Cyril telephoned Montgomery and Lionel's parents. Then she went back to her room.

"Your parents are coming to fetch you," said Sapphire. "I expect they will be very pleased to know that you are both safe. Promise me you will never do such a silly thing again."

Lionel and Montgomery both promised.

CHAPTER 7

Pearl had a wonderful idea. It was decided that the school children would put on a goodbye concert for Great Grandma and Mincemeat. The concert was to be held in The Old Town Hall. The town hall was a huge lobster pot. There was a stage, and lots and lots of rows of shell seats facing it, with comfy cushions on all the seats.

There were all kinds of instruments that the children would be playing. The shrimps would play the violins, which were made from old wood and string from fishing nets. The small fish would make up the trumpet section, and their trumpets were made from curly sea shells. The small crabs would play the drums, which were old saucepans turned upside down. The rest of the children, the limpets and mussels, would play guitars made from old frying pans and small fishing rods. Montgomery and Lionel were so excited to be playing in the school concert, and hoped very much they could sit together, and that teacher Pearl would put them in the front row.

Everybody was invited. The concert was to start at 6 o'clock. Soon the town hall was packed, and there was not a seat left empty.

The music was extremely loud! Great Grandma and Mincemeat were special guests, and had front row seats. Great Grandma loved the loud music and was jumping up and down in her seat, and clapping in time to the music! Mincemeat, however, was not so keen on such a loud noise, and decided to put his ear muffs on.

All the children in the orchestra were rocking backwards and forwards in time to the music, and the small crabs were beating the drums as hard as they could!

Sparkling seaweed juice was served to everybody at the end of the concert.

The next morning after breakfast, Mincemeat packed all the luggage into the submarine. It was time to get home. There was gardening to be done, and Mincemeat was very excited to try out a new recipe for his baking!

Everybody turned out to wave goodbye to Great Grandma and Mincemeat, and, as he steered the submarine through the big door in the rock, Mermaid Milly blew Mincemeat a special kiss.

GREAT GRANDMA GOES INTO SPACE

CHAPTER 1

As you know, Mincemeat, Great Grandma's exceptionally lovely large ginger cat, loved cooking, especially baking!

Today though, was different. Mincemeat was not going to do any baking. Mincemeat was going to build a space ship!!

Firstly, he would have to know how. Really he needed an instruction book. Mincemeat searched through all the kitchen cupboards and drawers for his library card. *Oh galloping grasshoppers,* he thought to himself, *wherever have I put it?* He searched high and low, and still could not find it. *However am I going to build a space ship without an instruction book?* he said to himself. He scratched his lovely ginger head with his great furry paw. Just then he had an idea. He remembered going to the library last week to get a book out on cake decorating, and that he hadn't taken off his 'I Love Cooking' apron. Betty Bookfinder, the librarian, had remarked to Mincemeat what a lovely apron he had, and Mincemeat had beamed.

Mincemeat went to the broom cupboard where his apron was hanging on a hook. He looked in the pocket, and there was his library card with his name standing out in big bold letters – **Mincemeat.** Oh, he was so relieved to find it!

Great Grandma was in the garden as usual, doing some planting. Great Grandma loved her garden, and today she was planting a row of giant onions. She especially liked them fried with squashed tomatoes and crispy spiders.

Mincemeat opened the back kitchen door and called out to Great Grandma "I'm just going to the library, back soon."

He put his crash helmet on and his black spotted motor bike rider's suit, putting his library card in his suit pocket. Jumping on his motor bike, he drove carefully down the hill. Safely at the bottom, pressing the accelerator, he sped off along the lane.

Betty Bookfinder was rather like a long stick of spaghetti, but with arms and legs. She wore her glasses right on the end of her long thin nose. Betty was very fond of Mincemeat. Mincemeat approached Betty's desk. Betty was very happy to see him.

"Good morning Mincemeat" she said, smiling at him, "and what can I help you with today, is it another book on baking?"

"Good morning Betty. Oh no, it's not a cookery book I am after today. I am going to build a space ship, and I need an instruction book please," replied Mincemeat.

"Oh, how exciting!" said Betty. "Where are you off to?"

"To visit the Gobbleitups on Planet Gobble," replied Mincemeat.

"Oooh," said Betty. "That's the lovely bright green planet isn't it?"

"That's right," said Mincemeat.

"Now, is it a small, medium, or large space ship you want to build?" Betty enquired.

"I think, medium please," said Mincemeat. "Great Grandma and I will want to have room to take some luggage. The Gobbleitups have invited us to stay the night."

"Well, I have heard that it is really lovely on Planet Gobble, especially at this time of year, quite spring like," said Betty.

Betty Bookfinder walked over to a huge bookcase. She had to climb up onto a step ladder to reach the top shelf which had a notice on it that said 'How to Build a Space Ship'. She took down a large book entitled 'How to Build a Medium Sized Space Ship'. Coming down the ladder carefully, she handed Mincemeat the book.

"This should help you Mincemeat, it's got very good instructions and lots of pictures." Mincemeat followed Betty back to her desk where she stamped the book in black ink: **Please Return in Three Weeks.**

"Thank you so much Betty for all your help, see you soon, and I will send you a postcard from Planet Gobble."

Mincemeat put on his crash helmet, putting the library book safely in Great Grandma's handbag that she had lent him. He put the bag on his tail, and jumping on his motorbike, headed for home.

CHAPTER 2

The very next morning Mincemeat awoke early. He always slept in the cosy old red armchair next to Great Grandma's bed. Great Grandma was still sleeping, so Mincemeat went downstairs to make her a cup of tea as usual. Switching on the radio whilst he waited for the kettle to boil, he did a little twirl around the kitchen in time to the music, for as you know he just loved dancing.

Putting the tea cup on the wooden tray, with two dead fly biscuits which Great Grandma loved, he very carefully took it upstairs. Placing the tray on the rather rickety bedside table, Mincemeat shook Great Grandma gently, telling her that he had left her a nice cup of tea.

Back in the kitchen, Mincemeat had a quick breakfast of roast beef and tulip sandwiches left over from yesterday's lunch. Then he took the library book and went out into the garden shed. Opening up the book, he began reading. He turned the pages, and there, folded up neatly was **A Map of The Stars.** Mincemeat started to study it.

All that Great Grandma could hear was a great deal of banging, clanging and hammering coming from the garden shed. *Oh dear* she thought to herself, *I do hope that Mincemeat can manage to build the space ship.* Great Grandma was always ready for an adventure, so when Mincemeat had suggested to her one evening, whilst sipping their dandelion cocoa sitting by the fire, that they visit the Gobbleitups on Planet Gobble, she thought it was a splendid idea.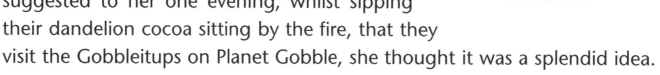

"It's rather a long way, Mincemeat," Great Grandma had said. "Do you think I should write to The Man in The Moon to see if we can stop off half way for tea and a rest?"

"That's a jolly good idea, because then we can refuel the space ship," replied Mincemeat.

So Great Grandma wrote to The Man in The Moon, telling him of their plans.

Mincemeat worked day and night building the space ship. Great Grandma was getting quite worried that he would wear himself out, but he was very determined to get it exactly right, and followed all the instructions in the book. She would often hear him singing along to the radio.

One morning, Great Grandma found Mincemeat frantically searching all the kitchen drawers.

"Whatever are you doing?" she asked.

"I am trying to find my cake baking kit" he said. "I need it for the space ship."

"Didn't you put it in that old large empty biscuit tin, the one you had left over from the lovely birthday gift that Aunt Petunia sent you?" asked Great Grandma.

"Oh sizzling sausages!" exclaimed Mincemeat. "However could I forget!" He fetched the step stool, and carefully climbed on it to reach his tin which was on a rather high shelf. Climbing back down, he tucked the biscuit tin under his arm and disappeared back into the shed. In the shed, Mincemeat kept his old sewing machine that used to belong to his grandma. He had some material left over from when he had made the curtains for the sitting room. Mincemeat set to, and made two sets of curtains for the space ship. Great Grandma heard the patter of the sewing machine and wondered what on earth Mincemeat was up to.

Three days later, Mincemeat asked Great Grandma if she would like to see the space ship, for it was all finished. Mincemeat told Great Grandma to close her eyes and then he opened the door of the shed.

Great Grandma could not believe her eyes, for there in the sunlight stood the most magnificent space ship that Great Grandma had ever seen. It was silver and red. Mincemeat had covered the space ship in very very thick

silver and red icing. He had decorated it with silver balls left over from his cake decorating. Mincemeat showed Great Grandma around inside. He had made the whole of the inside from marzipan. The dials on the flight deck were old baking tins. Great Grandma thought it was amazing! The engine was astonishing! It was made from six giant fruit muffins and was powered by dandelion juice!

"What a truly wonderful achievement!" declared Great Grandma. "I am so so proud of you Mincemeat" she said, and she threw her arms around him and kissed him on his very lovely furry face. Mincemeat beamed, and puffed out his chest with pride.

CHAPTER 3

Great Grandma and Mincemeat decided to travel the day after next. Mincemeat started getting everything organized. He wanted to take an especially nice present for The Man in The Moon, and started looking in all his cookery books for a nice recipe to make. He decided he would make his most favourite recipe, cream buns. Wanting to make them extra special, he went out into the garden to pick some yellow and purple crocuses to go into the mixture.

Soon the most beautiful smell filled the cottage, and Great Grandma went into the kitchen to ask him what he was baking. Mincemeat had been spooning the lovely gooey mixture into star shaped bun cases. Having whipped the cream ready to fill the buns, he was now licking the large wooden spoon with the remains of thick cream on it. His gorgeous furry ginger face was covered in cream! Great Grandma thought he looked so funny, and knowing how much he loved cream, she stood there and laughed! Mincemeat didn't mind, and started laughing too!

Whilst the buns were baking, Mincemeat went out to the shed to fill the fuel tank of the space ship with dandelion juice. Then he made sure all the lights and all the dials and switches on the flight deck were working. Finally he tested the 'Launch' button. Everything was working splendidly. Opening the big shed door, Mincemeat then got into the driver's seat of the space ship. He carefully drove the space ship out of the shed and into the garden ready for their journey.

Going back into the kitchen, and putting on his oven gloves, Mincemeat very carefully lifted the buns out of the oven. When they were cool, he filled them with the lovely whipped cream. He then wrapped them up in silver paper, tying the parcel with a huge pink ribbon to give to The Man in The Moon. Great Grandma in the meantime was out in the garden picking dandelions and nettles. She took them in to Mincemeat, who then baked two lovely loaves of dandelion and nettle bread to take to the Gobbleitups.

Great Grandma went upstairs to pack her best blue jumper and skirt which matched her very sparkly blue eyes. She put her jumper and skirt in the suitcase, together with Mincemeat's best orange waistcoat that he only wore for very special occasions. After all, they were going to Planet Gobble to visit the Gobbleitups!

CHAPTER 4

The next morning bright and early, Great Grandma and Mincemeat climbed into the space ship. Mincemeat put Great Grandma's suitcase in the cupboard he had made inside the space ship, along with the presents for the Gobbleitups and The Man in The Moon.

Mincemeat climbed into the driver's seat and helped Great Grandma to sit in the seat next to him. They both put on their space helmets and fastened their seat belts. Mincemeat switched the engine to 'Go'. It started up with a rumble. Then he pressed the 'Tilt' button. The space ship slowly lifted upwards until it was pointing straight up into the sky.

"Oh, how exciting!" squealed Great Grandma as Mincemeat pressed the 'Launch' button. The engine roared! The six giant fruit muffins that made up the engine, whizzed round and round faster and faster! The dandelion juice powered up the engine! Louder and louder the engine roared and suddenly the space ship, shaking vigorously, lifted up off the grass and into the sky!

Mincemeat steadied the spaceship, and soon they were going through the clouds, climbing higher and higher. Gradually the sky turned from light blue to dark blue.

"We're in space!" shouted Mincemeat to Great Grandma, who clapped her hands together excitedly.

The stars were so bright and twinkly. The space ship moved slowly through space. The sky was like velvet. Mincemeat got the Map of The Stars out.

"We need to turn left at the next big twinkly star, then right, and then straight on for the moon," Mincemeat told Great Grandma.

They turned left at the big twinkly star, and it seemed they were travelling for quite a long time.

"I hope we haven't gone wrong," said Mincemeat, when all of a sudden there was a sign in the sky which said **TO THE MOON STRAIGHT ON** with a big arrow. Mincemeat turned the space ship to follow the arrow.

As they approached the moon, Mincemeat could see a landing strip. As he looked down, he could see The Man in The Moon smiling and waving. Then Mincemeat saw a sign which said 'Park Here'. Slowly he lowered the space ship and steered it into the parking space. Great Grandma and Mincemeat took off their space helmets and undid their seat belts. Mincemeat helped Great Grandma out of her seat and opened the door of the space ship. As they stepped out onto the moon, The Man in The Moon was waiting for them.

The Man in The Moon spoke in a very slow deep voice that sounded like warm treacle. "I was so happy to get your letter telling me of your visit. I have been looking forward to it so much," he said. "What a magnificent space ship!"

"Thank you," said Mincemeat. "I built it myself."

"Oh, how clever you are!" said The Man in The Moon.

Mincemeat beamed, and handed him the present of cream buns they had brought with them.

"Oh, thank you so much, I didn't expect a present," said The Man in The Moon. "Do come with me, I have tea all ready."

Great Grandma and Mincemeat followed him a little way from the space ship. There, on the surface of the moon, was a tablecloth made from sunbeams. On the cloth was a beautiful cake, and a plate of biscuits. There was also a large jug of moon squash.

"Please sit down," said The Man in The Moon, pointing to a rug he had spread out next to the tablecloth.

Great Grandma and Mincemeat settled themselves on the rug, and The Man in The Moon poured them both a glass of moon squash, and cut a large slice of cake, first for Great Grandma, and then for Mincemeat.

"What a delicious cake!" Great Grandma and Mincemeat both said at the same time.

"Thank you," he said. "I made it from stardust, especially for your visit." Then, offering them the plate of biscuits, "These are moonbeam biscuits, would you like to try them?"

They took one each, and both agreed they were the most delicious biscuits they had ever eaten.

"I just love baking," Mincemeat told The Man in The Moon. "Would I be able to have the recipes?"

"Of course, it would be my pleasure," The Man in The Moon replied. "I read in your letter that you are off to Planet Gobble to visit the Gobbleitups."

"Yes, that's right," replied Great Grandma.

The Man in The Moon chuckled. "Oh, I think you are in for a surprise there!" he said, "but they are lovely little people, and I am sure they will make you most welcome."

Soon it was time to continue with their journey, and Mincemeat asked if he could refuel the space ship.

"Of course you can" said The Man in The Moon. "I have a fuel pump right by your space ship. It is very good fuel, it's Milky Way juice."

Mincemeat opened the fuel hatch on the space ship and filled it up until the dial on the flight deck said 'Full'. Then he thanked The Man in The Moon and kissed him. The Man in The Moon gave Mincemeat the recipes for the stardust cake and the moonbeam biscuits, and a little box to each of them.

"What is in here?" asked Great Grandma.

"Those, my dear, are Moonbeam Kisses."

"Thank you so much, we will treasure them," said Great Grandma, "and thank you for a most delicious tea."

The Man in The Moon was beaming as he waved to Great Grandma and Mincemeat as the space ship took off. *What a lovely day I have had,* he thought to himself, as he closed his eyes and fell fast asleep.

CHAPTER 5

Meanwhile, on the other side of the galaxy, there was great excitement on Planet Gobble. Preparations were being made for Great Grandma and Mincemeat's visit.

The thing about the Gobbleitups was that they just loved eating! They were shaped like fat little aubergines!

They were getting ready a magnificent feast for Great Grandma and Mincemeat. They had been busy for days! There were pies and cakes, jellies and ice-cream, trifles and chips, sausages and pizza, and lots and lots of spaghetti!

The Gobbleitups lived in the woods on Planet Gobble. They were spreading the feast out on long wooden tables under the trees. There was a lot of giggling going on amid all the preparations!

High above them, Mincemeat was following the Map of The Stars. They had to keep going until they reached the smallest star of all. The space ship travelled along smoothly, following the stars. Then, there in the distance, was a sign in the sky which said:

**PLANET GOBBLE
TWO STARS AHEAD**

"We're nearly there!" Mincemeat said excitedly to Great Grandma.

They gradually came closer and closer to Planet Gobble. It was indeed bright green, just as Betty Bookfinder had said. Then they saw buildings, and a sign which said:

GOBBLE AIRPORT FOR SPACE SHIPS AND FLYING SAUCERS

As Mincemeat began to steer the space ship slowly down, he could see a huge sign which said 'Landing Site' with spaces marked out. One said 'Fuel' and another said 'Launch Pad'. Next to that was a sign, 'Parking For Space Ships', where there were two already parked. Another sign said 'Parking For Flying Saucers'. Mincemeat carefully brought the space ship down and parked next to the two other space ships. In the next space, a flying saucer was just taking off.

The Gobbleitups had seen the space ship land and they all gathered round, chattering in very squeaky voices. Mincemeat opened the door of the space ship and helped Great Grandma out. The biggest Gobbleitup said that everybody was so happy to see them. Great Grandma said how lovely it was to finally be on Planet Gobble, as she handed him the present of the two loaves of dandelion and nettle bread. He was delighted!

Great Grandma and Mincemeat were quite tired from their long journey, so they were taken by the biggest Gobbleitup to their hotel, Gobble View, for a rest before going to the feast. The biggest Gobbleitup said he would come back to collect them in two hours' time.

After a short nap, Great Grandma woke up refreshed. She put on the blue jumper and skirt she had packed to match her sparkly blue eyes. Decorating her hair with pearls, she put on her best pearl earrings.

Mincemeat put on his best orange waistcoat reserved for special occasions. They both looked extremely smart. Downstairs in the hotel, the biggest Gobbleitup was waiting for them.

No time was wasted in getting to the feast in the woods. Great Grandma and Mincemeat travelled along to the feast in the bottom half of an old flying saucer driven by the biggest Gobbleitup. The seats at the feast had been made from the bottom half of old flying saucers too. They were astonished when they saw all the wonderful food that was laid out before them.

Great Grandma and Mincemeat were quite thirsty by this time, and as they sat down to enjoy the feast, a small Gobbleitup brought them two glasses of ice-cold planet juice. It tasted most delicious and rather like popcorn.

When everybody was full up from all the delicious food, and quite sleepy, the biggest Gobbleitup took Great Grandma and Mincemeat in the flying saucer car to their hotel, Gobble View, for the night. The hotel was a giant flying saucer and had wonderful views all over Planet Gobble. They could even see the landing site where their space ship was parked.

Great Grandma and Mincemeat were so tired by this time, after all the excitement of the feast, that they fell into their beds, which of course were made from old flying saucers with lovely snugly duvets on them. Soon they were both fast asleep.

CHAPTER 6

Great Grandma and Mincemeat awoke early the next morning, for it got light very early on Planet Gobble. They went downstairs for a delicious breakfast of fried eggs on galaxy toast, and planet juice to drink. Then they went upstairs to pack their things. Great Grandma stopped to admire the view out of the window. She could see the landing site, but couldn't see the space ship.

"Mincemeat," she said, "I thought you parked the space ship in the parking space marked 'Space Ships'."

"Yes, of course I did, Great Grandma," Mincemeat replied.

"Well," she said, "I can't see our space ship."

"It must be there, it can't have disappeared overnight!" said Mincemeat.

But the space ship had disappeared overnight!

Now, do you remember that when Mincemeat had built the space ship he had covered it in silver and red icing? And do you remember that he had made the whole of the inside from marzipan? And do you remember that the engine of the space ship was made from six giant fruit muffins? And, do you remember my telling you that the thing about the Gobbleitups was that they just loved eating?!

Oh yes! The Gobbleitups had indeed gobbled the space ship right up in the middle of the night!

Just as Great Grandma and Mincemeat were wondering whatever could have possibly happened to their space ship, there was a knock on the door. Mincemeat opened the door, and standing there was the biggest Gobbleitup.

"May I come in?" he asked.

"Of course," said Mincemeat.

"I am afraid I have some news for you, and I am not sure how to tell you."

"Whatever is the matter?" asked Great Grandma.

"Well," he said slowly, "in the night some very rascally business occurred. I am very sorry to tell you, but your space ship has been gobbled right up!"

Nobody spoke for a moment. Then Great Grandma started to laugh. Mincemeat started to laugh. The biggest Gobbleitup started to laugh. Soon all three of them were laughing until their sides ached!

When Great Grandma caught her breath, she said "But how do we get home?"

"Oh there is no problem there," said the biggest Gobbleitup. "I shall take you home myself in my brand new shiny whizzy flying saucer."

"Well, if it's not too much trouble, that would be wonderful," said Great Grandma.

"It would be my absolute pleasure, and the least I can do," said the biggest Gobbleitup. "I am really sorry about what happened."

"Oh, please don't feel bad about it," replied Great Grandma. "When we stopped off for tea with The Man in The Moon on the way here, he said that we might be in for a surprise!"

That evening, by the light of the moon, the flying saucer landed in Great Grandma's cottage garden.

"Would you like to come in for some supper?" she asked the biggest Gobbleitup.

"That is very kind of you," he replied, "but I really must be getting home."

"Well thank you," Great Grandma said, "for bringing us home," ".....and for the wonderful time we had," added Mincemeat.

Great Grandma and Mincemeat stood in the cottage garden and waved goodbye to the biggest Gobbleitup as the flying saucer took off. He gradually disappeared from view, flying past The Man in The Moon on his way back to Planet Gobble.

On a very clear night, if you look closely enough when the moon is a **full** moon, you will see The Man in The Moon. His face will always be smiling down at you.

That, I can promise.

CPSIA information can be obtained at www.ICGtesting.com
Printed in the USA
BVIW12n1711090817
491572BV00002B/58

9 781628 574593